River Traffic

River Traffic

Martha Brack Martin

orca soundings

ORCA BOOK PUBLISHERS

Library and Archives Canada Cataloguing in Publication

Martin, Martha, 1967–, author
River traffic / Martha Brack Martin.
(Orca soundings)

Issued in print and electronic formats.
ISBN 978-1-4598-1336-6 (paperback).—ISBN 978-1-4598-1337-3 (pdf).—
ISBN 978-1-4598-1338-0 (epub).

I. Title. II. Series: Orca soundings
PS8626.A77255R58 2016   jc813'.6   c2016-900546-1
                           c2016-900547-x

First published in the United States, 2016
Library of Congress Control Number: 2016931883

Summary: In this high-interest novel for teens, Tom gets involved in smuggling
on the Detroit River while trying to save the family marina.

*Orca Book Publishers is dedicated to preserving the environment and has
printed this book on Forest Stewardship Council® certified paper.*

Orca Book Publishers gratefully acknowledges the support for its
publishing programs provided by the following agencies: the Government
of Canada through the Canada Book Fund and the Canada Council
for the Arts, and the Province of British Columbia through
the BC Arts Council and the Book Publishing Tax Credit.

Cover image by iStock.com

ORCA BOOK PUBLISHERS
www.orcabook.com

Printed and bound in Canada.

19 18 17 16 • 4 3 2 1

This book is for my
first family, the Bracks,
and my second family, the Martins.

The former gave me dreams to dream,
and the latter are my dreams
come true. I love you all.

Chapter One

I had only seconds to spare. The other machine was right on my tail. If I turned too soon, I'd be dead.

I squeezed the throttle and pulled ahead a few more meters.

I risked a second glance back at the other Jet Ski in my wake. It was closing in! I carved the water as I swung my machine to the right...

And suddenly I was airborne.

I felt the yank on my life jacket as I flew off, taking the ignition key with me. Then a shock as I hit the cold river water.

Coming up, I checked on my machine. It was nearby, bobbing in the waves. Nate held the steering wheel. He didn't look as thrilled as I thought he would. After all, he'd just won our race.

"You beat me! Why aren't you happy?" I yelled. Nate was looking past me, over my shoulder.

I whipped my head around.

Dominik Oleg, the biggest jerk in the world, was in a sleek speedboat idling just behind me. His ride must have cost at least $80,000. He looked down at me as I bobbed in the water.

"Of course he won." Oleg smirked, moving his boat closer as Nate brought my Jet Ski over. "You could never win any race with that piece of crap, LeFave."

"He could have if you didn't swamp his machine!" Nate yelled over the motor.

"Hey, I can't help it if your friend doesn't know how to drive, Murphy. Maybe you shouldn't hang around with losers. Stick with the guys on the team."

Just because Oleg was the quarterback, he thought he could tell the rest of the team what to do. Especially the younger ones like Nate.

"I can pick my own friends, thanks."

I was glad to see Nate wasn't backing down. I just hoped Oleg didn't make him pay for it later.

"Whatever." Oleg pointed at my Jet Ski. "Did you borrow that from your daddy's dumpy marina? Bet no one else wanted it."

"Shut up, Oleg. At least I paid for my machine myself. I didn't need my *daddy* to buy it for me."

Oleg's eyes flared. I knew I'd hit a nerve.

"You don't know what you're talking about, LeFave. I'm making so much *bank* right now, I don't need my father to buy me anything. And it's only gonna get better," he bragged.

"Yeah, sure it is. 'Cause you're a high roller. In your mind at least," I said.

"Listen." Oleg pointed at Boblo Island behind him. I could just see the row of million-dollar mansions through the trees on the shore. I knew he lived in the biggest one. "You boys are playing in *my* backyard. And you're way out of your league." He suddenly honked his boat's horn, scaring the crap out of Nate and me. His grin was a nasty threat.

"Don't play with the big boys. You won't like how the game ends."

Chapter Two

I had lots of time to think about my run-in with Dominik Oleg the next day after school. I was volunteering at the LaSalle police station. I did it every Monday after school for a couple of hours. Nate's dad was one of "LaSalle's finest." He knew I needed the hours to graduate.

"Are you still only able to help out Mondays, Tom?" Nate's dad asked.

"Yeah, sorry, Officer Murphy. Dad needs me after school at the marina the other days. At least until winter." Working for Dad at our marina didn't pay well—or at all—but he needed me. We were struggling as it was. Since Mom left, Dad's heart wasn't in the business.

That's why Oleg's cracks really bugged me.

"You let me know if things change. You're a good help around here."

"That's nice of you to say. But I know I don't do much. I try though."

"I always knew you'd do well here." He looked around the new station. "You're a kid who pays attention. You'd make a good cop."

"Thanks." I could feel a big grin take over my face. "I love helping out here. I get to hear what's going on. It's interesting."

"It is, at that. People think a small town like ours has nothing happening. But we have our share of crime."

"Maybe it's in our blood. Because of our rum-running history, I mean." I grinned.

LaSalle really took off in the 1920s and early '30s. That's when Prohibition made it against the law to buy or sell booze. Canadians could still make it though. Most of our area got in on the smuggling of Canadian booze to Michigan. Our marina is built on one of the creeks my dad's family used for sneaking whiskey across the river.

"I'm not sure our history has much to do with it," Nate's dad said, smiling. "Our town is growing fast. It's not surprising people find a way of getting into trouble."

"I guess. You guys seem to have your hands full with speeders and small-town stuff."

He laughed. "We don't tell you everything, you know." Then he got more serious. "Listen. You know how I said you were good at paying attention?"

"Yes, sir." I wondered where this was going.

"Nate told me you boys were out on the river yesterday." Was Officer Murphy going to lecture me about racing with Nate?

"With the weather still so nice, the traffic on the river is almost as busy as in summer. We could use some more eyes out there." I must have looked confused, because he went on. "Just let me know if you see anything unusual."

"Okay, sure. I can do that."

"Around your marina too. I mean, you're right on the river there." He was looking at me closely. "Have you noticed any strangers?"

"No, sir. We aren't exactly super busy. New people would stand out."

"Okay," Nate's dad said. "I've said this to Nate too. But we both know he's about as observant as mud." We laughed as he headed back to his office.

Soon it was time for me to leave. I grabbed my backpack and said goodbye to the dispatcher. As I walked through the outside door, Officer Murphy popped his head around the partition.

"Just remember what I said, Tom." He paused. "Keep your eyes and ears open around the river."

Chapter Three

Saturday morning at our marina isn't exactly busy. I wanted to sleep in, but Dad expected me to be on the job at eight. Since Mom left, he'd been staying up later and later. In the last couple of months he'd started working in the old shed at the waterfront. At least, he says he's working. I'm not allowed to go out there anymore, so who knows?

I don't smell booze on him or his clothes, but I wouldn't be surprised if he's slugging back a few out there. He's in such a cranky, crappy mood all the time, I'm not willing to push my luck and explore.

Our marina still has regulars, but they're mostly locals who've kept their boats here for years. Dad's always been a great mechanic—he can fix anything—so that draws a few customers too. Still, the fancier marinas have all the bells and whistles. We don't usually get much traffic.

That's why I was amazed when a Carver 43 Super Sport pulled into our channel. She was incredible! I wished Dominik Oleg could see her parked in our marina. She put his boat to shame. I estimated she was worth close to half a million.

The sun reflected off her bimini cover, so I couldn't see who was driving.

I expected the yacht to reverse any second. I wasn't stupid—our marina wasn't up to the standards of a boat like that.

I couldn't believe it when the pilot moved the Carver into docking position.

I ran and tied up the rope on the bow. As the pilot shut off the engine, I moved to the stern. I was just reaching to grab its mooring rope when I heard footsteps.

That's when I got my second surprise.

A pair of long, curvy, suntanned legs started down the steps—and I almost stopped breathing. The legs were followed by cutoff denim shorts that fit *really* well. Thank God the owner of those legs didn't see my face before I realized I was standing there, stunned, with my mouth wide open. I snapped back to reality just in time to close it before the rest of her came into view.

"Hey there!" the girl said in a cute Southern accent. She was smiling from ear to ear with this great smile I knew would haunt my sleep for days. She couldn't have been older than seventeen or eighteen. She pointed at the mooring rope I still held. "Thanks for giving me a hand. I'm Kat. Well, really Kathleen. But no one calls me that except my dad." She put out a tanned hand for me to shake.

"Hi. Welcome to LeFave's Marine and Repair." I gestured behind me with a little *ta-da* motion and tried not to look embarrassed. "I'm Tom LeFave."

"Well, it's nice to meet you, Tom LeFave." She pointed at the yacht. "Can we get a docking slip for the *Southern Comfort* tonight?"

I didn't know what to say. We had plenty of empty slips. She could see that with her own eyes. But why did she want to dock her beautiful, pricey boat at our small marina? The *Southern Comfort* was way too classy for LeFave's. Just like she was way too classy for me.

I guess I took too long to answer. She raised her eyebrows (which I noticed were as perfect as the rest of her.) "Is there a problem, Tom? Aren't you open?"

"No problem. We *are* open. I just…" I paused. Dad would kill me if I let her and her amazing boat get away. "Are you sure you'll have everything you need here? I mean, we do our best, but we're pretty small. No bar or restaurant or pool."

She smiled that amazing smile again. She looked relieved. "Your spot here is perfect. I really want to check out the local rum-running history. I'm kind of a history buff. I wanted to dock close to town. Then I could explore on my bike before we continued up the river."

"Oh." I shrugged. "Okay then. And you're right. You're in the middle of local history. Our marina land was actually used by rumrunners back in the day. The creck was already here. My shady ancestors just improved it."

"That's amazing! So you come from a long line of bad guys?" *Was she actually flirting with me?*

Before I could answer, we both heard noises coming from the cabin of the *Southern Comfort.* We turned in time to see a bald, angry-looking guy shove open the glass door that led to the cabin of the yacht. He was huge—solid—and at least six foot four. He scanned the marina in one quick glance. Then his eyes squinted as they found mine.

"Where in thc hell are we, Kathleen? *And who in the hell is this*?"

Chapter Four

"Daddy!" Kat looked embarrassed. "That's no way to say hello!"

Daddy? This scary guy was someone's father? *Kat's* father?

"How was your nap?" she asked.

He wasn't about to be distracted. "Kathleen, where are we? What have you been up to while I've been sleeping?" His Southern accent wasn't as strong as Kat's. He still looked angry, but at least he wasn't growling or swearing anymore.

"This is LaSalle, Daddy. On the Ontario side of the Detroit River. We're just north of Boblo Island." Kat's dad started to speak, but she put up a hand to stop him. "I *know* you wanted us to dock at Boblo. But I really wanted to check out the rum-running history here."

"You and your history." He smiled. It made him look less scary.

"We can move on to Boblo in a day or two. You aren't due before then, right?" Kat's dad shook his head. "I thought if we stayed here, I could take my bike tomorrow and ride around. Check out the town."

Kat's dad stopped smiling right away. "You are *not* going biking around a strange town on your own, Kathleen! And I can't take you." They shared a funny look. "You know what I've got going on."

"What if I found someone to take me around?"

I'd seen enough girls at school trying to get guys to do what they wanted. I knew a pro when I saw one. Kat clearly knew how to work her dad. "This is Tom LeFave. His family owns this marina."

Just like that, I was part of her plan.

"Hi, sir. Nice to meet you." I offered him my hand. I was kind of afraid he might snap it off. Even though I was supposed to be hanging out with Nate the next day, there was no way I could let Kat down. Nate would totally understand. It wouldn't be polite to leave her on her own. Or friendly. Or smart.

Did I mention she was perfect?

"I'd be happy to take Kat…er… Kathleen around town, sir. I can show her all the historical spots. LaSalle is a very safe town. And we have bike paths."

Kat threw me a grateful look.

Her dad did not.

"Are you sure you aren't just stringing me a line? We don't know anything about you."

"There's not much to know, sir. I live here. I'm sixteen. I get good marks, and I play hockey."

"Are you any good?"

"I'm all right."

Kat's dad gave a big sigh. "We can talk about it more tomorrow," he said.

Kat looked happy, so I figured that was a yes, even if he didn't say it. Then he gave me a scary look again. "And if I do say yes, you'd both better be back here by five," he added.

"Absolutely, sir."

"Now Kathleen, since we're going to be here for the night, let's pay and get supper going. You've got your school-work to do, and I've got a few calls to make tonight."

Kat turned to face me. "I'm being homeschooled. Or boatschooled, I guess."

She smiled again. "Dad has to travel a lot for work. Since I wanted to come, I said I'd do my courses for eleventh grade online."

Eleventh grade? I couldn't believe she was the same age as me. She looked older for sure.

Before I could ask her where home was, her dad cut us off.

"Come on, Kathleen. I'll go pay and you can get started on the cooking. And Tom, I'd appreciate it if you'd hook us up to the marina's pump-out station."

Kat smiled apologetically as she turned to board the *Southern Comfort.* We'd both been given our orders. She was cooking. I got to empty the bathroom tanks.

"See you tomorrow?" she asked. "How's 9:00 AM?"

"Perfect."

By the time I got finished all my marina chores, our Saturday-night pizza was waiting for me. Dad was in the office, talking on the phone. I was inhaling my fifth slice when I realized Dad's voice was getting louder.

"I have to do this, Joe. I need the cash, and I need it fast." I had no idea who Joe was. And I knew all of Dad's friends.

I found myself getting up to listen more closely, even though I knew it was wrong.

"If I can't pull this off, I could lose the marina." His voice dropped. "And I can't lose it, Joe. It's not just my job. It's Tom's home. We'd be out on the street."

Holy crap! I had no idea things were that bad. What was Dad trying to do? I knew the marina wasn't bringing in a lot of cash, but we always seemed to scrape by. He sounded so worried.

My mind raced as I tried to think what to do. Maybe another part-time job?

Dad's sigh brought me back from my thoughts. His voice was just a whisper on the wind as I strained my ears to listen.

"The marina is all we have left, Joe." He paused. "And I'll do whatever it takes to keep it."

Chapter Five

I tossed and turned all night, trying to figure out what was going on with Dad and the marina. He had sounded so desperate. Not like himself at all.

I gave up trying to sleep when the sun came up. I dragged my tired body through my chores. I figured I'd clean the front office while I waited for Kat.

Maybe I'd find clues about what was going on.

By nine I'd come up empty, and Kat was at the door.

"Hey there. Are you ready to show me LaSalle's rum-running past?" Kat said. She had this way of flipping her ponytail when she talked. I almost missed her words because my brain was stuck on how amazing she was.

"Sure. I am. I mean, let's go." It was hardly a smooth opening. But it got us out the door.

Our marina was one of many along the Detroit River between Old LaSalle and Amherstburg. Most were bigger and fancier, but ours was one of the oldest. It had been in our family for years.

We rode our bikes along the highway that followed the river. Kat was full of questions.

"So did Al Capone really come to LaSalle in the '20s? I thought he was based in Chicago."

"He definitely came to LaSalle. Windsor too," I said. I pulled up at the Tim Hortons. "In fact, there are stories that he stayed in that house right there." I pointed across the road at a three-story mansion. It was now owned by one of LaSalle's history buffs. "And Mae West, that blond actress who used to tell guys to *Come up and see me sometime*? They say she performed there too. The guy who built it liked to bring in big names to impress his guests." I pointed up to the third floor. "The top floor was where shows happened. He also had quite a few working girls who had little rooms on the second floor. The bad guys dropped by when they came to make deals."

"No kidding. Sounds like *Boardwalk Empire*! Did anyone die with all these gangsters around?" Kat asked as she snapped pictures with her phone.

"Not that I know of. Not in that house anyway. But lots of smugglers got killed on the river. There are stories of shoot-outs over loads of booze. One group of bad guys stealing another group's stuff. Some rumrunners got killed by the law."

"I bet it wasn't easy to catch them."

"Especially when half of the local cops were probably in on it." I laughed. "The Chateau and the Sunnyside were both operating back then." I pointed at the Sunnyside Tavern, now up for sale. "They were speakeasies. Secret rooms and everything."

Kat looked like I'd offered her a present.

"Can we get into them?" she asked.

"Not today. If we had more time, you might be able to get the real estate agent to show you around." I shrugged. "There's a bar in Windsor called Abars that was a big rum-running spot back in the day. It's still around. Too far to bike though." I grinned. "If you came back in the summer, we could go on the rumrunners tour they offer in Windsor. And if you can talk your dad into staying longer, I could show you Hiram Walker's mansion. He's the guy who made and sold Canadian Club whiskey. He created a whole town from the money he made."

"We're only here for a week. And that's out on Boblo Island. Dad has business meetings there. We have to leave tonight."

Figures. I finally meet an awesome girl, and she's just passing through. It bugged me even more when I thought of her on Boblo. It wouldn't take Dominik Oleg long to spot her. At least she wouldn't be impressed by his boat. Hers was better!

"I'll give you my cell number," Kat went on. "Just in case we can work something out."

With school, the marina and volunteering, there was no way I'd have time to get together during the week. Still, it was a nice offer.

"That would be great," I said. We grabbed donuts and drinks and sat while I continued my tour guiding.

"Most of the town got into the smuggling business one way or another. It paid a lot better than growing radishes."

"Radishes?"

"That's what LaSalle was famous for before Prohibition."

"Well, smuggling sure sounds a lot more exciting than radish farming." Kat smiled. "With all that overgrown shoreline, hiding stuff must have been pretty easy. And with the States just across the river? It had to be pretty tempting." Kat was silent for a minute, deep in thought as she drank her iced coffee.

"Do you think there's any smuggling

going on around here these days?" she asked.

"For sure at the border. They're always pulling in people at the bridge and at the tunnel to Detroit."

"Nothing around here though?" Kat said. "No drugs? Illegal aliens? It seems like it would be really easy to bring stuff across."

"There was a guy who hired a local fisherman to sneak some people over to Detroit. I just read about it in the paper. In fact, the fisherman first met the guy in charge at Abars. Kind of ironic." We both laughed. "That's the only time I've heard about people being smuggled. We aren't exactly the border between Mexico and Texas."

"I guess. So how did the police catch the guy?"

"Our local cops have a boat. Mounties and customs officers too. Though you don't see them around much."

"Well, at least you've got them. And the States probably has their guys too." Kat looked thoughtful. "Ever see any US lawmen in the water around here?"

"Can't say I have. Doesn't mean they aren't there. But none of our regulars have mentioned it."

As we got back on our bikes and headed for home, I thought about what Kat had said. It would be pretty easy for smugglers to move stuff if no one was looking. How could cops be everywhere on the water? Was this what Officer Murphy was talking about when he said to watch for anything out of the ordinary?

And then it hit me. Kat's yacht was definitely out of the ordinary. And her dad sure didn't look like some casual boater. She *did* explain why they were here—but there were lots of other marinas in the area. Other marinas that were more suited to their pricey yacht. I still didn't know what kind of business her dad was doing on Boblo. He sure didn't seem like a three-piece-suit kind of guy.

As Kat turned and smiled at me, I told myself I was crazy. There was no way she was anything but what she seemed— pretty and amazing and honest.

Even if I still didn't know her last name.

Chapter Six

It took me a few minutes of riding before I got up my nerve. "Hey, Kat. What's your last name?"

She looked surprised at my question. "Smith. Didn't I tell you when we met?"

"No. We somehow missed that part." It was Smith. No mystery. Just Smith. "Where do you live when you aren't traveling with your dad?"

"Oh, here and there. We've moved a lot." Kat started pedaling faster. "Race you back to the marina!" she yelled over her shoulder. And that was the end of my questions.

When we got back home, I could see Dad was in the office. He had a frown on his face as usual. Kat's dad was on the yacht, clearly watching for our return. He didn't look much happier. Kat gave him a little wave as we walked with her bike down to their boat slip.

"Give me your phone and I'll add my number," Kat said. We swapped phones. "Thanks so much for taking me around. I really loved it. I'll call you if I can figure something out. For this week, I mean."

"Absolutely. Anytime." I wanted to say something funny or impressive, but I kept thinking about Dad looking upset. "Have a good time on Boblo. It was great meeting you." I turned to go.

"This is how we say goodbye in the South." Kat leaned forward and gave me a hug. "You take care now."

Did I mention she was perfect? She smelled perfect too. Even after a sweaty bike ride in the sun. I saw her dad glaring at me from the deck of the yacht. I let go of her in a hurry.

"You take care too. Have fun on Boblo. It's full of history. It used to be a big amusement park, for one thing."

"Yes, I read that. I'll check it out."

I wondered how long it would take her to run into Dominik Oleg. They'd both have boats docked in the same marina. It was a small island. The thought of Oleg anywhere near Kat made me want to punch him in the face. Even more than usual.

"Tom! I need you!" Dad's yell brought me back to reality. I gave Kat a final wave and ran back to the office.

When I got in I could see Dad's desk was a mess. I wondered if his bad mood was because he knew I'd been looking around.

"What's up?" I asked.

"I can't find this paper I need. I thought I left it here last night. Were you messing around with my desk today?" Dad sounded more bugged than angry.

"I tidied up a bit before I left with Kat. What was on the paper?" I moved closer to the messy pile on the desk. Dad's body slid in front of me, blocking me.

"Just a letter I got." Dad's voice made it clear I'd better not ask any more questions. "Forget about it. I probably filed it already." He shoved all the papers together in a big pile and hugged them close to his chest. When they were all gathered, he looked at me. "How was your day with Miss Kathleen?"

"Great." It felt like years since Dad had been interested in talking to me about normal stuff. "I showed her around town. She was really curious about the rumrunners."

"You sure she wasn't just curious about *you*?" Dad raised his eyebrows up and down. "She's quite a beauty."

"She *is* pretty amazing, isn't she?" I could feel the goofy grin on my face. "I wish they'd stay here longer."

"I wish they needed some pricey repairs." Dad's smile was a little forced. But it was still more than I'd seen in weeks.

Just then the phone rang. Dad's smile was gone in a flash. He shooed me outside, so I wondered if it was Mom. He kept his voice too low for me to hear.

About ten minutes later I was on the dock when I heard the office screen door slam shut. I was gassing up one of our regular customers' boats. Dad came around the corner, walking with fast, sharp steps. He headed toward the shed by the water.

I don't know what I was thinking. Maybe it was having Dad back to normal before the phone call happened. Maybe I wasn't thinking at all.

"Hey, Dad? Why don't I fry up some bacon and eggs for dinner? We aren't too busy. We could watch some baseball after we eat. Hang out for a bit."

Dad's steps didn't slow. He didn't turn his head. His steps took bites out of the path to the shed.

"Dad? Did you hear me?" Nothing.

I tried a new tack.

"Do you want me to bring your dinner to the shed?"

That made him turn around in a hurry.

"Don't you come anywhere near the shed! I'll get dinner when I'm ready to eat!" He pointed his finger at me. "Remember, the shed is off-limits to you." He yanked open the shed's side door. The inside was a dark mouth. "In fact, you stay inside tonight. I don't want you roaming around out here. I can handle the dock."

He must have seen my face, because his voice softened. "No reason for both of us to get eaten alive by the bugs." He grabbed the shed door to close it behind him. Then he paused for one last comment.

"Promise me you'll stay inside, Tom. I mean it."

Chapter Seven

Monday mornings are never fun. Accidentally sleeping in just makes them worse. My sleepless Saturday night was bad enough. Tossing and turning over Dad's weird warning on Sunday meant I lost more sleep. I guess that was why I didn't hear the alarm. Thankfully, I had my bike. There was no way I'd ask Dad to drive me.

I was just turning in to the school parking lot when I heard a screech of tires. I whipped my head toward the sound.

A muddy wall of water met me, face-first. I hit the brakes on my bike. Then I wiped at the water dripping down my face. My neck. My whole freaking body.

"SUCKER! You can't stay out of the water, can you, LeFave?" Dominik Oleg yelled. I could hear his laugh as he zoomed off. His Mustang's tires were dripping. I knew he'd hit that puddle on purpose. I was drenched in the previous night's rain.

I locked up my bike and dragged my soggy butt into school. Luckily, my locker was right around the corner. I grabbed my gym clothes and ran to change. I made it to my Sports Leadership class right as the bell rang.

"Why's your hair wet?" Nate asked. He pointed at my legs. "Is that mud?"

"Oleg," I said. "He made sure I was fully awake."

A supply teacher walked in and started setting up. We had some time.

"I wish I knew why that guy is such a psycho to me. What did I ever do to him?"

"Yeah, he really does seem to hate you." Nate thought about it. "You're a year younger, but you aren't scared of him. You don't care that he's a big football jock." He laughed. "He's not used to that. Maybe it really bugs him."

"There has to be something more. You aren't scared of him either."

"Yeah, but I'm not as popular as you." I must have made a face, because Nate argued. "It's true. Everybody likes you. Teachers. Kids. You have that good-guy/leader thing going on. Oleg puts up with me because we're on the football team together. He can't go after me. It goes against his code of honor."

"Yeah, 'cause he's so honorable." I rolled my eyes. "You and I are both in this leadership class. And people like you just as much as they like me."

"Maybe. But I'm not as good in school as you are. And the only way Oleg's ever going to get an A is if he 'buys a vowel.'"

I had to laugh. Oleg was no student, for sure. He almost couldn't play football this year because he failed math last year. It got around the school fast. Lucky for him, the principal cared more about winning than following his own rules. He let Oleg play, but Oleg had to get tutoring. He was taking eleventh-grade math again this semester. Sadly, he was in my class.

"I'm sick of him," I said. "I'd like to punch him in the face. But then his dad would probably sue me. Or Oleg would win." I paused. "Maybe both."

"Just stay away from him," Nate said. "It sucks that you've got to see him in math every day."

"It's too bad his dad can't buy him good grades. He buys him everything else."

I thought of my dad, struggling to keep our marina afloat. Oleg's boat was worth more than my dad made in a year.

"Rumor has it his dad cut him off after he bombed his classes last year. His dad is old school. Eastern European. Oleg's supposed to follow in the family business. Failing is not an option." Nate took a moment to flip his hair out of his eyes. "I think it really bothered him when you chirped about his dad buying his boat for him. He made a big deal at practice about telling us he's making his own money. Said he'd be making a lot more soon too."

"Yeah." I nodded. "He said that when he swamped me. I'd like to know what he's doing to make all that cash. Did he say? I could really use a job like that."

"Nope. Just bragged that it would be coming in faster than he could spend it."

The supply teacher was waving her arms, trying to get our attention. "All right, leaders. It's time to get started," she said.

As we began running drills, I couldn't stop thinking of Oleg. Maybe he was working for his dad. The family business had to be doing well if they lived on Boblo. That seemed the most likely. He wouldn't want to admit it. It would look too easy. Like his dad was still just giving him money.

Everyone ran off to shower at the end of class. Thanks to Oleg, I didn't have any other clothes.

I went outside to wait and decided I'd pay a little more attention to Dominik Oleg. I'd try to find out if he really had a job. There was something going on with that guy. I could feel it in my gut.

And I wouldn't let him sneak up on me again. If nothing else, I'd stay drier.

Chapter Eight

I worked at the LaSalle police station after school. I apologized for showing up in my gym clothes. The dispatcher just laughed, but I felt like a loser. When Nate's dad showed up an hour later, I apologized again. He was more interested in anything I had to tell him.

"Nate mentioned you had a girl from the States staying at your marina,"

Officer Murphy said. "A girl in a super expensive yacht. All Nate could tell me was *she's hot*."

I groaned. "Nate didn't see her. And I didn't describe her like that. I mean, yeah, she's pretty, but she's also really nice. Funny and smart too."

"I can see why you ditched Nate yesterday." He smiled, but his eyes stayed serious. "Where's she from? Did she say?"

"I asked, but she never really told me." I realized that was kind of odd as I said it. "She and her dad are traveling for his business. They're at Boblo now. They only stayed the one night with us."

"What kind of business is her dad in?" Officer Murphy asked. I admitted I didn't know that either. He looked even more interested. "What did you guys talk about? Did they take you onto their boat?"

I smiled to let him know I could tell he was grilling me.

"Kat Smith is her name," I began. "I don't know her dad's name. He has meetings on Boblo for the next week, so they're staying there. I *did* think it was kind of strange they stopped at our marina—their boat was way more high-end than we usually see."

Officer Murphy jotted down what I told him on his tablet. I went on listing my observations.

"The yacht is called *Southern Comfort*. I didn't get on it at all. It's a Carver 43 Super Sport. Not brand-new but close. Probably worth about half a million," I finished.

Nate's dad was really smiling now. "Not bad, rookie. Anything else?"

"Kat said they stayed at our place because she was interested in the rumrunners. She had me take her around town to show her everything."

Nate's dad studied what he'd written.

"So she asked a lot of questions about our area then?"

"She did. But they made sense. She was curious about how much smuggling went on today. But I couldn't tell her much." I shrugged. "I really think she's honest. Her dad is a scary guy though. Big. All muscle. He doesn't look like a businessman."

"Interesting. Any chance you have their boat registration number and can look it up for me?"

All boats have a code made of letters and numbers, like a license plate. The registration shows where the boat normally docks.

"Of course," I said. "I meant to look it up myself. I forgot once we started hanging out."

"Not surprising if she's as hot as Nate says." He grinned. "I'll follow this up. In the meantime, keep your eyes peeled.

Watch for anyone acting weird. There are rumors something big is heading our way. And soon."

I wondered what he meant. "Something big?" I asked.

He nodded. "We've been told to be extra watchful. If you see anything that doesn't look right, give me a call on my cell." He gave me his personal work number. "Don't get involved on your own though." He put his hand on my shoulder. "I mean it, Tom. You're like another son to me. Call if you need my help."

His face was very serious. He raised one eyebrow. "Remember, you're still just a kid, even if you *are* a smart one." Officer Murphy gave my shoulder a pat and walked out the door.

As I rode home from the station that night, I kept replaying what Nate's dad had said. Kat and her father were definitely out of the ordinary for LeFave's Marine and Repair. But I wondered if Nate's dad was hinting at more. I thought of his comment about me being like another son. Was he trying to tell me something else?

There was someone I knew who was acting very weird. Someone who was desperate for money. Someone who didn't want me near our shed by the water.

I couldn't help but wonder.

Was Officer Murphy warning me about my own dad?

Chapter Nine

Dad kept acting weird all week. Maybe I was just more aware of it, thanks to Officer Murphy's warning. It was a relief to go to school each day.

I had a chance to study Oleg every day in math class. That was the one place where he acted like I didn't exist. I was almost disappointed. I wanted to see what he was up to. I watched him sweat as he got more and more lost in math, but that wasn't helping me figure him out. I asked Nate to keep an eye on him at football practice. They were together after school every day. Chances were good he'd hear something.

I was spending another weeknight in the house, away from the river and Dad's shed. I thought I'd go crazy. Then, after dinner, Nate texted me:

Oleg having big party this Sat. on Boblo.

Back-to-school bash.

Whole team invited.

I texted back:

U going?

Nate replied:

Figure I better. ☹

I typed:

No prob. U will have 2 check out his place 4 me. See what's up.

Nate answered:

Will keep eyes + ears open.

Knowing Nate would get to check out Oleg's house should have made me feel better. Nate was no superspy though. If a pretty girl was anywhere near him, he'd be useless.

I was dying to get into the Oleg supermansion myself. No way would I ever be invited though. It would be all seniors and football guys. And I couldn't forget Oleg's warning when we were racing near Boblo. He didn't like me on the river in his "backyard." He'd be really mad if I made it through his front door.

Maybe I could borrow someone else's boat and check out the party from the water.

I was plotting how I could swing that when I got another text.

Hey there, Tom. How r u?

It was Kat. I tried to play it cool.

K. U?

She answered:

Been checking out history here.

Not a lot 2 c anymore.

Cool spooky buildings tho.

She sent me some pictures she'd taken of the old ruins on the island.

I wrote:

Great shots.

I was thinking about Officer Murphy wanting to know more about Kat and her dad. I'd learned that the *Southern Comfort* was licensed in the Florida Keys. Was it worth asking Kat more questions?

My phone's incoming text tone went again. She wrote:

Met a guy over here.

I forgot about the *Southern Comfort* pronto.

Why was Kat telling me about another guy? It's not like we were a thing. At least, I didn't think so.

Did totally wishing count?

Before I could decide what to answer, she texted again:

U might know him. He goes 2 school in LaS.

Crap! I knew right away who it had to be. Oleg! And of course she'd pick him over me—who wouldn't? I didn't have two bucks to rub together. Dominik Oleg was rich and a football star. And he had that damn boat!

I was so worked up, I almost missed her next texts:

I hope he's not ur friend.

He's an idiot.

Dom Oleg.

For a moment I was speechless. Kat *had* run into Dominik Oleg on Boblo, just like I had expected—and she could tell right away he was a jerk.

Awesome!

I texted:

He IS a jerk. Did he talk about me?

She texted back right away:

No. Didn't talk 2 him much.

Asked me 2 come 2 party @ his place Sat.

There was a pause between texts. Then:

Wanna come w/me?

I think my brain froze. Of course I wanted to go to a party with Kat. I'd want to go anywhere with Kat. The fact that the party was in Oleg's super-mansion made it even more appealing. The problem was…how could I go? Oleg would take one look at me and throw me out. Literally!

I texted back:

Oleg h8s me.

No sense sugarcoating it. Kat texted back:

Gr8. He's trying 2 impress me.

I could believe that.

She added:

Won't do anything if u come as my d8.

And he'll have 2 keep his hands off!

The thought of Oleg with his hands on Kat made my blood steam. I pushed the thought away. Could I be this lucky? A date with Kat *and* a chance to spy on Oleg?

I texted:

I'm in. Should b fun.

Kat offered to pick me up in her yacht. I said I'd run myself out. We hammered out a time and place to meet—Boblo Marina at eight o'clock. We could walk over to Oleg's super-mansion from there. I gave her one last chance to back out.

I texted:

U sure ur up for this?

Her message came back fast.

Yes! Can't w8! ☺☺☺☺

I stared at the row of smiley faces. I tried to tell myself the spying option was a bigger deal than spending time with Kat.

Too bad I didn't believe it.

I'm going on a date with Kat. She *asked* me. *We're going to a party in a Boblo supermansion. Oleg's super-mansion. And I get to spy on him as an added bonus...*

Now if I could just figure out what Oleg was up to, avoid making a fool out of myself in front of Kat and—just for a change—not end up soaking wet...

Chapter Ten

Dad seemed really happy on Saturday night.

"It's about time you had some fun in your life," he said. "You'll have to tell me all about the Oleg place tomorrow. I bet it's something. Be sure to look around so you can give me details." He chuckled.

I realized I hadn't heard that sound in a long time.

I didn't tell him there was a good chance I wouldn't get past Oleg's front door, even with Kat beside me. Dad had offered to drive me over, but I wanted a quick getaway if I needed one. No way was I waiting for Dad to come get me if Oleg and I got into it. Dad was in a big hurry for me to get going. I figured he was itching to get to his shed. I wondered if that was why he was in such a good mood. An evening without me looking over his shoulder, wondering what he was up to.

We decided I'd take the marina's old runner. The forecast called for a storm later. The runner was pretty good in waves. Not much to look at, but Dad had her running faster than you'd think. I threw a towel over the seat so I didn't sit in anything. I was thankful the wind blew away the runner's fishy, oily smell.

In no time I pulled into Boblo Marina. I spotted the *Southern Comfort* right away. Kat was waving. Her hair was down. I couldn't help but notice that her white jeans fit as well as her denim shorts. She looked like a model.

"Hey there," Kat called. She welcomed me with another Southern hug. "I'm so glad you could come. I missed you."

"I missed you too. I mean..." *What did I mean?* I was so bad at this. "Thanks for putting yourself in the line of fire. Going with me and all. You sure you don't mind if Oleg throws me out?"

"He won't. And if he does, I'll have an excuse to leave too. I'm fine with that." She looked guilty. "I really just wanted to see inside his mansion. As long as he throws you out *after* I get a chance to snoop, I'm good!"

"To be honest, I want to look around too." We turned the corner onto the street with the biggest homes on the island. I wondered how much to tell her.

"Oleg's been telling everyone he's got this great job. One that makes him a lot of money. I'm curious," I said.

Kat nodded. "He told me that too. I thought he was just trying to look like a big shot. I think that's why he invited me. Trying to impress me. Or maybe his dad told him he'd better." Kat shrugged, grinning. "He did say he had some friends for me to meet. They're boating over from Grosse Ile. Wherever that is."

I pointed down the river. "Grosse Ile is the biggest island out there. It's really one huge island with a few small ones all around it. There's a bridge that joins it to the mainland. It's on the US side of the river. Very high-end. More super-mansions. He probably met his friends boating."

"Probably. He seems a little obsessed with that boat of his."

"You think?" We both laughed.

"I can't be rude to him. Our dads are doing business together. They're at a dinner meeting tonight."

I wondered again what Kat's father did. I didn't know a lot about Oleg's dad. Rich businessman. Multiple companies. Big into donating lots of money to local service groups and sports teams.

"Have you met Mr. Oleg?" I asked.

"Just this week. He seems like a nice enough guy. Not shallow like his son. He's a bit intense though."

"What do you mean?"

"He couldn't do enough for Dad and me when we got here. Invited us over and offered us anything we needed. Really warm and friendly. Then Dom came home. Oleg Senior got very stern very fast. No more smiles. All business." Kat shook her head. "I kind of wondered if something was going on between them. Dom looked almost scared of him.

He wasn't the same kid I'd met on the marina dock, bragging about his boat."

She pointed at two massive stone pillars guarding a wide, curving drive. "And on that note, we're here."

We walked up the drive, past a shiny Mustang. The last time I'd seen that car was through a puddle sliding down my face.

Music was pounding through the open French doors and windows. Kids were everywhere. I looked for Nate but couldn't see him outside.

Kat grabbed my arm, then slipped her hand into mine. She leaned in as we walked up the front steps. I was hoping it was a romantic move—I was all for it—but she had another purpose.

"Listen," she whispered. "If you get a chance, go explore. I can keep Dom busy. Just promise me you'll tell me what you find."

"No! I mean...that's not very gentlemanly of me. I can't just leave you. Unless I get tossed out the door, of course." I grinned.

"I'm serious." Kat's accent was stronger when she whispered. "We'll get in the door, make small talk, and then you can go snoop. Just don't leave me hanging for long." She squeezed my hand. Her eyes stared into mine. "I'd rather spend tonight with you than anyone else."

And that's when the front door swung open.

Chapter Eleven

I don't think I'll ever forget the look on Oleg's face when he saw me with Kat on his front step.

First he saw only Kat. His face broke into a big smile. His dimples and too-white teeth were flashing. You could almost feel the charm oozing off him.

"Miss Kathleen." His fake Southern accent was lame. "I'm so glad you could come." His eyes met hers. Then they moved from her face down to her feet and—very slowly—climbed back up. "You look smokin' hot."

Did he really just check out my date right in front of me?

Before I could do or say anything, Kat spoke.

"Thanks for inviting me, Dom. And thanks for letting me bring my *very* good friend." She kept our hands together, swinging them so Oleg couldn't help but notice. "This is Tom LeFave."

Oleg's eyes slid to my face. His look was priceless.

"Hi there, Dominik," I said cheerfully. "Thanks so much for inviting me." Holding hands with Kat, and seeing that look on Oleg's face, made me feel brave.

Oleg's hands were fists at his side. I could tell he wanted to tear me apart.

"LeFave." He looked back at Kat. She was smiling sweetly. "I didn't realize you knew Kathleen. I can't imagine how that could *ever* happen."

He didn't move. His body was blocking the entry to his house.

"Tom and I have some mutual friends," Kat said. "Al and Mae."

I almost laughed out loud. Al Capone and Mae West. Yup, we were tight.

"I understand you boys go to school together?" Kat made it sound like a question.

"Yeah. We don't hang out though. LeFave's just a kid. And he's *not* on the football team." Oleg said it like I had scales and three arms. He paused. "We *have* run into each other a few times lately though, haven't we, LeFave?" He smirked. "It's supposed to rain tonight. You don't want to get *wet* again."

Reminding me of our soggy run-ins clearly gave Oleg back his good mood. He moved out of the doorway and smiled again at Kat.

"Go inside and get a drink, Kathleen. Make yourself at home." His voice was all charm. "I'll be in after I tie down the patio stuff. Tonight's storm is almost here." He looked me right in the eye. "And you never can tell what *crap* a storm will toss up on your front steps."

Oleg made his way down the stairs. He turned back to face us at the bottom.

"You and I need to have a little chat, LeFave," he said, his eyes locked on mine. "I'm busy tonight, but don't you worry. We'll talk soon." His eyes narrowed. "That's a promise."

"Speaking of crap…he's full of it! Don't even listen to him," Kat said as we walked into the house.

"I know." At least I'd made it in the door.

We ran into Nate in the kitchen. He was trying way too hard to get some girl's phone number. We said hi but left him to it. I was happy to have Kat all to myself.

The party was pretty cool. Oleg was gone for a good hour. I forgot about snooping—it was so great to hang out with Kat. We were talking about music when Dominik showed up again. The fake charm was back.

"Miss Kathleen, how are you doing? Hope you aren't too bored." His look said she must be, hanging with me. "Remember I told you I wanted you to meet some friends of mine? They're your type of people." Oleg shot a look at me. "They're waiting for us by the fire pit."

Kat looked at me. Using her hair to block Oleg from seeing her face, she winked.

"Sounds good, Dom. I can't wait." She put her arm through his. "I'm sure Tom can find something to do while we're outside."

With Kat minding Oleg, I made my way through the partygoers, checking out rooms. One on the main floor was locked.

"Can't go in there, man. Dom's dad's office." A very drunk linesman from the football team was slumped on the stairs, watching me. "He locked it up before he left," he added.

"Thanks, man. I'm looking for a washroom." I pointed toward the kitchen. "That one's busy."

The linesman pointed upstairs behind him. "That way. Top of the stairs. Right beside Dom's bedroom."

I raced past my helpful tour guide. If anyone asked, I figured he'd back up my story. If he didn't pass out first.

I found Oleg's bedroom easily. The wall of fame with trophies, ribbons and photos was a big clue. The room was bigger than my whole home, with windows across one wall facing the water.

A giant map of the Detroit River was framed on another wall. There was a top-of-the-line Mac sitting on his desk. I kept low so no one could see me from outside and turned it on.

It booted up fast. Oleg's password was *football*—my second guess after his name. It was so obvious. But then, this was Dominik Oleg.

I checked out his email. There was nothing about any job. Nothing at all, really. I wondered if he had another email account. I couldn't find anything in the computer's history either.

The party was getting lively outside. I moved sideways behind a curtain to look for Kat. She was there with Oleg and three other kids. Probably the Grosse Ile crowd.

Oleg was practically sitting on her lap. He had an arm wrapped around her tighter than a rubber band. After seeing that, I decided I needed to move faster.

I shut down his Mac and left it as I'd found it.

Luckily, Oleg's trophies were illuminated by little pot lights. I used their glow to search through his desk. Then I tried Oleg's night table. Other than a large stash of football magazines, I came up empty.

"Something's got to be here. What about the closet?" I whispered to myself. I opened the door, letting the handle slide back into position slowly in my hand.

Oleg sure isn't a neat freak.

There were piles of clothes on the floor, even though there was a hamper right there. I flipped through the hanging clothes, searching for anything weird. I stopped when I came to a camo outfit. Pants, jacket...the whole thing. I wouldn't have pegged Oleg for a hunter. I checked the pockets. Nothing.

I was moving to check out his dresser when I heard a noise through Oleg's wall. The side opposite the bathroom.

Had some couple come upstairs to fool around? Not likely. I'd kept the door open because that's how I'd found it. No one had walked by.

Could they have been up here the whole time?

I slipped out of Oleg's room and moved to the room next door. I had my hand on the doorknob when I heard more noises from inside the room.

It would bug me if I didn't check it out.

I got my excuse ready in case a couple was inside. *Oh, sorry! I was just looking for a spot for me and my girlfriend.*

I pasted a smile on my face and gave the doorknob a good loud turn.

That's when I realized three things.

One, the door was locked from the inside.

Two, something was definitely in there, because I heard two more loud bumps.

And three, someone was slowly and quietly sneaking up the stairs behind me.

Chapter Twelve

There was no way I could get into the washroom before the person climbing the stairs saw me.

I tried anyway.

I stepped toward the washroom just as Kat's blond head came into view.

"Tom, do you know where the restroom is?" Kat asked loudly. "The ones downstairs are full."

She mouthed, *Are you done?*

"It's right here," I said just as loudly. Silently I tipped my head at the locked door down the hall and mouthed, *Locked.*

Kat pulled me into the bathroom and shut the door behind us. "We have to get back downstairs. Dom's inside," Kat said. "Everyone is. The storm's really picking up. Dom thinks the ferry won't run if the waves get higher. People are leaving."

I nodded but took time to fill her in on what I'd found. "I hate to go without knowing who or what is in that other bedroom," I whispered. "Don't you think it's weird no one ran to open the door when I tried the handle? Or said anything?"

"I guess whoever it is doesn't want to be found," Kat said.

I nodded. "Yeah. And *I* guess we'd better get out of here."

Kat peeked through the door to make sure no one was there. Then she grabbed my hand and we walked downstairs. Hopefully, people would just think we had been fooling around. The front foyer was packed with kids grabbing coolers and purses and shoes.

"It was great meeting you, Kathleen!" A tall kid dressed in namebrand everything smiled at Kat as he pulled on expensive boating shoes.

"Nice meeting you, Troy," Kat said. "You too, ladies," she added. Two cute brown-haired girls smiled back. "These are Dom's friends from Grosse Ile. Troy Heron and his friends Megan and Emma. They belong to the Grosse Ile Yacht Club." She pointed at me with her free hand. "This is my friend Tom LeFave."

"Nice to meet you, Tom. Sorry we can't stay. The river's getting crazy out there. We're going to leave while we still can," Troy said. They headed out the door.

"If it's that bad, I should get going too," I said. "I wonder where Nate is. And where's Oleg? Shouldn't he be here saying goodbye to his guests?"

"I'll go find him to say thanks." Kat looked at me. "Why don't you wait on the street?"

I remembered Oleg's threat about talking later. "Good plan. Just don't take too long."

Kat left to find Oleg. The rain was crazy. The temperature must have dropped about five degrees in the last twenty minutes. The sky was an angry blackish-green. I could see the river between the houses. It was a sea of whitecaps.

I wondered if Nate had left already. I'd thought maybe I'd get a ride with him instead of taking the runner home. Most kids who had driven over on the ferry had parked their cars at the end of the street. I didn't see Nate's.

Kat ran up. "I can't find Dom anywhere." She shrugged. "I'll give him my thanks tomorrow. Right now we need to get back to the *Southern Comfort*."

We ran back to Boblo Marina as rain lashed our faces. I wondered if Dad was worrying about me. I checked my phone as I ran. There was no text or missed call.

The *Southern Comfort* was a warm, dry relief after the rain. Kat's dad wasn't back yet. I was relieved. The guy still scared me. I wondered how he'd feel about Kat and me being here alone.

Kat threw me a towel. We both dried off as much as we could. Our clothes were soaked.

"I'm sorry I don't have anything for you to change into, Tom," she said. "I've turned the cool air off. Want a hot drink?"

"No, don't worry about me. You go change. I might as well stay wet. I'll just get wetter in the runner."

"I don't think you should leave yet. The river's really rough. Dad should be home soon. Then we can take you back in the *Southern Comfort* when the storm's past. Or you can sleep in here on the pull-out sofa."

"I don't want to impose," I said. I saw that Kat was shivering. "Listen, go change into dry clothes. We can talk about it after you're warmed up."

Kat went to change. I made myself think about something other than her undressing not far away.

I couldn't imagine staying on the same boat as Kat's dad, having a happy little sleepover. Still, the river *was* crazy. I wondered if the runner was up to it. It was heavy and solid, sure. But it was open to the wind and rain. Visibility would be tough. At least Dad had it running fast.

I pulled out my phone again. Still no message from Dad.

I tried to call his cell. It went to voice mail. The same thing happened when I tried the marina landline.

Where in the hell are you, Dad? Why can't you get to a phone?

I wondered if Dad was so worried about me he was on his way to Boblo. But he would have called or texted first.

I messaged that I was on the *Southern Comfort*. The screen said *Delivered*. If Dad didn't have his phone with him, he'd see it later.

I paced around the cabin, waiting for Kat. There were worse places to be a confused, worried mess.

The Carver was as pretty inside as it was out. The shiny woodwork was a dark cherry. The furniture was covered in leather. I could see the galley had a wood floor and a full-sized fridge. Behind the eating area there was even a built-in bar.

Kat popped up, looking dry and perfect. I felt even more like a drowned rat.

"I can't get my dad on his cell or on the marina phone," I blurted. "I'm kind of worried."

"I'm sure he's fine. He probably fell asleep," she said. "If it's any comfort, I can't get my dad either. And he never goes anywhere without his phone." She looked out the window. "Maybe it has to do with the storm. Anyway, I'm sure he'd want you to stay here." She gave my shoulder a squeeze. "My cell's working fine, and I checked the satellite forecast. This storm won't blow over for another hour or two."

She showed me her phone. I could see we were in the most intense part of the storm right now. I decided to relax and stop worrying.

"Yeah, I guess I'd better stay put for now. My dad's likely fine. And I know he wouldn't want me to be out on the river in this. It's too dangerous. Even a big boat would have trouble."

"Good." Kat yanked up the tabletop and pulled a blanket out of the storage area in its base. "Here. Wrap up in this," she said as she threw it at me. "I want to hear again what you found upstairs." She sat down on the couch and patted the leather beside her.

There was no place in the world I'd rather have been than sitting beside Kat Smith in her pricey yacht, just the two of us. Talking about Dominik Oleg, however, was not a recipe for romance. I quickly repeated my story.

"So you didn't find any strange notes or papers in his desk? Nothing about money?" Kat asked. I noticed she had a cute way of tipping her head to the side when she was really thinking.

"Nope. Nothing out of place at all. Only the camo suit. And for all I know, he duck hunts. People do that around here." I felt stupid, like I should have found something. I was so sure he was doing something shady. "The only really weird thing was those noises in the room next door," I said. "There's only him and his dad living in that house."

"Don't you think it was probably just some kids from the party?" Kat asked. "Maybe they went upstairs before you got there."

"I guess. It just felt…sneaky." I tried to explain. "You'd think when I tried to open the door they would have yelled or something."

Kat was quiet for a second. "Maybe they were too…busy."

She laughed softly. It sounded different from her normal laugh. Slower maybe. She put her hand on my arm.

"I hear duck hunting isn't the only thing people do around here." She was looking at me with that little eyebrow-lift thing. "Or radish growing," she said more softly. Her face moved closer to mine. "Or rum-running," she whispered.

Is this really happening?

I knew I was staring at her lips. I couldn't help it. I tried to be cool and relax.

"Really?" I whispered, leaning to close the last little bit of space between us. "Did you read that in your research…?"

Just as our lips finally made contact—and I forgot to breathe again—I realized I was hearing more than the pounding of my heart and the storm.

I would have ignored it. But Kat pulled away. She did the eyebrow-lift thing again as we both listened.

There was no doubt about it.

Someone was revving a boat motor loud enough to wake the dead. That could only mean someone was about to tackle the river in this storm.

The question was who—And why?

Chapter Thirteen

Kat flew to slide open the cabin's glass doors. We raced up the molded stairs to the flybridge. The *Southern Comfort* was bigger than most other boats in Boblo Marina. With our 360-degree view and the loud roar, we spotted the other boat in seconds.

"That's Dom's boat," Kat said.

"Even *he* wouldn't be stupid enough to go out in this storm," I said.

"It's his. That's where he docks it. But that might not be him driving." Kat grabbed the binoculars resting nearby but soon threw them down. "Too much rain. I can't see his face."

Whoever was in Oleg's boat was putting on a life jacket.

"Why would he be heading out in this storm?" My gut said there was no good reason.

"We've got to follow him. But we can't do it in the *Southern Comfort*." Kat was almost shouting over the rain. "If that's Dom, he'll know it's us."

"We can take the runner." As soon as I said it, I knew it was a crazy idea. The runner was open to the wind and the rain. Waves too. We could be swamped if I made one wrong move.

Kat had seen the runner earlier. "Are you sure? Maybe we'll just have to let him go." She looked at the blurry figure, now moving to the stern mooring line. "I wish my dad was here."

I thought about Officer Murphy telling me to keep my eyes open but not get involved. I knew he wouldn't want me on the river. Dad would ground me for life—assuming I was still alive to ground.

I didn't even want to think about what Kat's dad would do to me if something happened to her.

"I'll go on my own. You can tell your dad when he gets back. You said he'd be here soon. You can be the cavalry."

I could see Kat's mind going a mile a minute. I wasn't sure she heard me, she was thinking so hard. Then she seemed to snap out of it.

"Nice try. You aren't going anywhere without me. No one boats alone in a storm." She grabbed a paper and pencil. "I'll leave a note for Dad downstairs. We'll put on life jackets and be fine.

The lightning's moved on. And you're going to need another pair of eyes in this rain." Kat pointed at Oleg's boat, now with one mooring line untied from the slip. "We'd better move fast. That boat's leaving soon."

I took the life jacket Kat handed me. We raced down the stairs.

I didn't have time to call Nate's dad from the *Southern Comfort*. And there was no way he'd hear me over the storm if I called from the runner. We had to get going or we'd lose Oleg's boat. I decided to send him a quick text while Kat went into the galley to write the note to her dad.

We got the life jackets on super fast. I handed Kat my phone in case Nate's dad texted back.

"Stay down," I shouted into Kat's ear as we dragged ourselves through the rain to the runner. "Don't let whoever that is see you."

Oleg's boat was pulling out of the slip one dock over. We jumped into the runner.

"We'll follow, but I don't want to get too close," I yelled. "I bet we're the only two boats on the water tonight. I'm keeping my lights off. They won't do much in this storm anyway."

The runner started right away. I was thankful Dad kept it in such good shape.

Oleg's boat was going south, a good two hundred metres ahead of us. It followed the narrow spit of land that separated us from the Livingstone Channel and the rest of the river.

"Where do you think he's headed? Kat yelled back. She was checking her phone and mine.

"I don't know! I can't figure out why he's going south!" I yelled. "It's out of his way if he wants to get across the river fast. Easier to go north and take the "Hole in the Wall" just north of Boblo."

Kat nodded. "Safer too. Going south takes him right to Lake Erie—and taking on the lake in this storm would be suicide!" The wind caught my words and threw them back.

The waves were getting worse by the minute. Oleg's boat was doing better than mine. As he came to the end of the spit of land, he turned east. I let out a breath.

"He's heading across the river after all!" I had no time to say more, because we were suddenly being tossed around like a cork. It was all I could do to keep the waves at the right angle to the runner. Kat put the phones in her pocket so she could hold on better.

"Anything on the cells?" I asked. She shook her head.

Out in the middle of the big channel, the wind was crazier than ever. I had to keep zigzagging just to move forward a few meters. There was no point trying to talk. We could barely see. There was no room for mistakes.

Sugar Island was close. It would block a lot of the wind and currents once we got behind it. But until we did, every wave was a risk. I was holding on to the wheel so tightly I couldn't feel my fingers.

Up ahead, Sugar Island loomed out of the downpour.

Suddenly Oleg's boat took off!

Kat whipped her face in my direction. I nodded to show I'd seen it.

Crap!

If I upped my speed before I got around Sugar Island, we were almost certain to swamp. If I didn't speed up, we would probably lose sight of Oleg's boat.

Both of my choices sucked.

And I was out of time.

Chapter Fourteen

I knew this whole risking-our-lives thing would be pointless if I didn't speed up. But I also knew the river.

The only logical place Oleg's boat could go from here, in this weather, would be Grosse Ile. Anything else was too far and risky.

I hated to do it, but I kept the runner steady until we rounded Sugar Island.

The River Fates must have been in a good mood or something. As I passed south of Sugar Island, the rain let up enough for us to see Oleg's boat in the distance. With a whoop, I let the runner fly full throttle.

The lights on Oleg's boat made it easy to follow him, especially when the rain got even lighter. The waves were calmer. The sky was dark, but it seemed bright after the storm.

There was no question that Oleg's boat was heading to Grosse Ile. It slowed down as the southeast island shoreline came into view.

"Maybe he's heading to the Grosse Ile Yacht Club," I said. I thought about meeting Troy earlier. "Do you think it might be Troy driving Oleg's boat? Maybe he stayed behind when the others left." It was a relief to be able to talk without screaming over the storm.

"No. They left right after we said goodbye. And they were on Troy's boat. He *did* say he lives just down from the yacht club though. Maybe Dom's visiting them. If it *is* Dom, I mean." Kat was scanning the shoreline closely.

"In a storm? Right after they were at his place?" I shook my head. "We're missing something."

Oleg's boat went right past the yacht club, keeping close to shore. I kept the runner back, trolling with our lights still off.

"Watch for channel markers," I said.

Kat nodded.

Up ahead, Oleg's boat slowed to a crawl. It kept following the shore, past huge multimillion-dollar estates lined up one after the other. Some had their own docks and boat lifts out front.

"I don't think he knows we're following him," Kat said.

"I don't think he ever did," I said. "Now he'll just assume we're locals if he does spot us."

I hope.

Whoever was driving Oleg's boat was clearly looking for something on the shore. The rain had turned to a light mist. I could easily see the driver standing at the wheel, turning his head as he looked around. But I couldn't see his features.

Oleg's boat glided by twin docks with huge spotlights shining into the channel. The driver turned from the lights. But for a split second we saw him clearly.

"It *is* Dom!" I said. "He's wearing that camo suit I found in his closet."

Oleg's boat suddenly went dark. I wondered if he'd heard me.

Oleg glided past a few more estates. Then he turned the bow and pulled up at a dock ahead of us. I brought the runner as close as I dared. I stopped two docks before the one he had picked.

What's he doing? Kat mouthed, scanning the shore. I shrugged.

We could see fairly well, despite the mist. Oleg was still looking around. We didn't see anyone on the dock or shore near him.

He made a quick wave with his arm.

Kat dug her phone out of her pocket and began taking pictures. This turned out to be a good idea, because something was rising out of the back of Oleg's boat. A big something. And I wouldn't have believed it if I wasn't seeing it with my own eyes.

Oleg went up to the large *something* and grabbed at it. A big tarp came off in his hands. We could now see two figures crouching low in the boat.

"They can't be leftover party guests. You don't hide *them* under a tarp," I whispered.

Kat shot me a look that clearly said, *Shut up*!

We couldn't hear what Oleg was saying, but his actions were clear. He wanted those people off his boat. They held back, huddling like they were afraid. Finally, one climbed out, then turned to help the other. Oleg wasted no time tossing two large bags out after them. The people grabbed the bags, holding on to each other, and quickly moved off the dock. We lost sight of them when they got to the shore.

I looked at Kat. I thought she'd be as confused as I was. But she didn't look it.

I turned back as Oleg began loudly stomping around in his boat. He still scanned the shore. He looked mad.

What's he waiting for? I mouthed at Kat.

She shook her head and mouthed, *No idea.*

Then, on the dark shoreline, I saw a figure carrying something. I thought it might be one of the people who'd just gotten off the boat. Then I saw that this person was much taller. Heavier too. Solid.

We watched as he stepped onto the dock. He walked right up to the boat and stood looking down on Oleg in silence.

"What took you so long?" Oleg's voice carried over the water. He sounded more freaked out than angry.

"Do you have the other delivery?" We could hear the tall man's voice just as clearly. Out of the corner of my eye, I saw Kat lean forward.

Oleg bent down and grabbed something near his feet. "Here." He almost shoved it at the tall man. "Now give me my cash. I wanna get out of here."

"Not so fast. I need to see if it's right." The tall man fiddled with the package. "You didn't open it?"

"No! Why would I? I don't want to know what's in there." Oleg sounded like a scared little kid. Not like the tough guy he pretended to be. "I'm just doing a job." He was loud, like he'd forgotten where he was. "I'd never do this if I didn't need the cash. I know it's wrong. But I'm desperate. Pay me and let me go."

The tall man tossed the bag he'd brought into Oleg's boat. He was silent for another minute.

Oh, crap. What's he waiting for?

I had a bad feeling our night was about to get worse.

Then the big man spoke.

"Don't you want to count it... Dominik?"

"No. It's fine. I'm sure—" Oleg stopped. "What did you say?" He looked up at the man on the dock. "How do you know my name?"

"I know a lot about you, Dominik." The tall man spoke loudly and clearly.

He put the bag Oleg had given him over his shoulder. Then he moved his free arm.

He's going for a gun!

I grabbed Kat, ready to yank her down, out of the line of fire. But the man flicked on a flashlight—one he aimed at his own face.

"And you know me, Dominik," he said slowly.

Kat and I gasped at the same time.

The tall man on the dock was Kat's dad.

Chapter Fifteen

"*Mr. Smith*?" Oleg looked as confused as I felt.

I glanced at Kat. Her face was frozen.

Should I get her out of here before it gets worse? Is it even safe to move?

Before I could come up with anything *close* to a plan, things got crazier.

A bunch of guys in bulletproof vests swarmed out of the dark. They charged onto the dock. Some of their vests said DEA. Others said FBI or US Border Patrol. They surrounded Oleg and Mr. Smith in seconds.

"Holy shit!" I was too scared to say it very loud.

I felt it louder, believe me.

We saw Mr. Smith drop to the dock and put his hands behind his head. I heard Kat let go of a big breath she must have been holding.

I looked at Oleg. He didn't say a word. Just stood in his boat like he'd been turned to stone. He looked so scared I felt sorry for him. Even if he was up to his eyeballs in something bad. Even if he had treated me like crap all through high school. I still felt bad.

And I felt even worse for Kat. Who wanted to see their dad taken down by armed guys in black?

I put my arms around her. She turned to face me and moved into my hug.

I held her for a few seconds. She leaned back. We stared into each other's eyes.

And her face broke into an ear-to-ear smile.

What the...?

I had no time to figure out how she could smile at a time like this. Stuff was still going down.

Huge spotlights suddenly lit up Oleg's boat and Mr. Smith. It was brighter than daylight.

The lights were coming from the channel—from three boats lined up, blocking Oleg in. One had US *Border Patrol* on it. Another said RCMP. The Mounties. The last one was turned so I couldn't see its logo. Then the guy driving it started waving at Kat and me.

So much for thinking we were hidden.

It was Nate's dad. He was driving the LaSalle Police boat. I could see Canada Customs agents with him.

He may be waving now. But he's going to kill me later.

The guys on the shore took Mr. Smith and Oleg into custody. The DEA guys pulled the money out of the boat.

I could hear Oleg muttering, "I'm so stupid. I *am* dumb…just like he said. Dumb Dom. Oh my god…" He kind of crumpled in on himself.

Some guy read Oleg his rights. Then they took him away.

The minute Oleg was out of sight, Kat leaped up.

"Come on. We're getting out of this boat." She tugged my arm.

"What?" I asked. "Your dad was just taken down by the cops! Why aren't you freaking out?"

"Don't worry about it. Get out of the boat," Kat said.

I felt like I was trapped in some crazy movie. I had to pry my hands off the steering wheel after our boat ride through hell.

I was sure we'd be taken down ourselves now that the cops had seen us. I needed a minute, so I stalled. I slowly took off my life jacket and carefully bent to stuff it behind my seat.

"Tom LeFave!"

I jumped a few meters as a deep voice barked my name.

Mr. Smith was standing beside Kat on the dock. His hands weren't cuffed. I looked for the cops, but he was alone.

"Sir." My voice cracked. "I mean…"

I had no idea what I meant.

I looked at Kat. She was grinning from ear to ear again. Her dad gave her a nod. "I'll let you tell him," he said to her.

"Daddy's FBI, Tom. High up. He was in charge of this whole thing," she said proudly.

Mr. Smith is FBI? My brain tried to catch up.

"I knew he'd probably be here," she said. "And I was sure I heard his voice on the dock. But he should have been running things behind the scenes. I couldn't figure out why he'd be doing the drop." Kat looked at her dad. "Why did you, Daddy?"

"Thanks to you two, we knew where to come. And we got here in time to move into position. But we didn't get a chance to completely secure the area," Mr. Smith said. "As lead, I felt *I* should take the risk, not my men. And once I knew our guy was Dom…" He put his arm around Kat. "I felt sorry for him, honey. I didn't know if he'd panic and do something stupid. If I was doing the drop, I hoped my guys might be a little less trigger-happy." He chuckled.

"What if Dom *had* panicked?" Kat said.

"I can handle myself. And I'll make a better witness for him at trial than one of my guys would. He said some things that might make a judge go easier on him."

I was still trying to catch up. I focused on the one thing that made sense to me.

"I knew you didn't look like a businessman, Mr. Smith," I said.

"The name's Waters. Agent Mike Waters." Kat's dad put out his hand to shake mine. Then he kept mine in his grip. "And *you* don't look like FBI. So I'm not sure why I'm not ripping you to shreds for bringing my little girl into this situation."

He waited to let me sweat a bit. Then he cracked a smile and let go.

"Maybe it's because I know my little girl," he said. "And no one can stop her if her mind's made up." He hugged Kat tightly. "Even if it almost killed me, knowing you two were out here somewhere. Between the storm and the drop, anything could have happened."

"So you knew we were following Oleg? Did you get Kat's note?" I didn't think he could have and still made it over here before us.

"I never wrote a note," Kat admitted. "He wouldn't have been home to get it in time."

"I'm lost," I said.

"Daddy was supposed to come back after dinner. When he didn't, I knew something must be happening. Then we heard Dom start his boat," Kat said.

I remembered what we were doing when we heard Dom's boat. I made myself focus.

"I had to give Daddy a way to track us if you and I were going after Dom," she said. "So I texted him when you were texting Nate's dad. I told him to follow the tracking chip he 'hid' in my cell phone." She rolled her eyes.

"Hey! I'm a dad," Agent Waters said. "We do what we have to."

"Well, most dads don't put tracking devices on their kids," Kat said. She looked at me. "I figured out Daddy put the chip in my phone when he gave it to me. I turned it off. But I had to turn it back on tonight. He needed to be able to follow us."

"I wondered why it looked like you never went anywhere after I gave you that phone. But it paid off. We tracked you and knew where Oleg was likely heading."

"Daddy tries to keep me out of his work. But sometimes I can get information he can't," Kat said proudly. "That's why I was at Dom's party. To check out the house. I hated to let you have all the fun. But someone had to keep Dom out of the way."

"I knew Kathleen would be safe with all those kids there. And with you of course," Mr. Smith—I mean Agent

Waters—said. "I had you cleared as soon as we met you."

"Super," I whispered. I wondered who had cleared me.

Kat's dad turned to her. "We got some intel late today from the new network. That's what put it all in play." He turned to me to explain.

"All the law-enforcement agencies in the area have been working together to set up a new network. It covers the river and lets us all talk to each other if there's a crisis. No middleman. No need for clearances and paperwork. It's state-of-the-art."

"All the agencies can share information the second one group hears about it," Kat said.

"We've had a few trial runs, but today was the real deal. A source confirmed that one of the Olegs had to be our guy. We just didn't know which one. Or the details,"

Agent Waters added. "You two gave us the one piece we were missing. And I can't thank you enough."

Agent Waters had us tie up the runner. Then we walked back to the big dock. All the action was winding down.

Kat pointed at a sign on the end of the dock. "*Heron's Nest*," she read. "Is this where Troy lives?" she asked her dad.

He nodded.

"Can we go home now, Daddy? I'm pooped," she said.

"You bet." Agent Waters waved to someone behind him. "I think Tom here knows his driver. We'll talk tomorrow." Kat's dad turned to me. "How about we meet at your marina around ten?"

I nodded as Agent Waters led Kat off. So much for a good-night kiss. She mouthed, *Good night*, and winked.

Officer Murphy walked up with another cop I knew.

"I won't tell you how I feel about you tracking the Oleg boy tonight," he said. "It's late, and we're both tired."

He walked me to the LaSalle Police boat and waited as I climbed in. "You're soaking wet. Grab a blanket and a hot drink. My thermos is right there. Jim will bring the runner home. Thank God that storm's done."

I wrapped up in a blanket. Before I could take one sip of coffee, I was asleep.

Chapter Sixteen

I woke up to Dad singing one of his favorite songs at the top of his lungs. He hadn't sung since Mom left. After all the stuff that had gone down the previous day, Dad's happy mood seemed even stranger.

When they'd brought me home the night before, he'd been waiting. Nate's dad must have told him we were coming. Dad didn't say where he'd been all night, and I didn't ask. Once I showered, he gave me a hug and sent me to bed.

"Tom! Get down here. I've made pancakes and bacon. Lots of bacon," Dad yelled.

And now he was singing and making me breakfast. Life was full of surprises.

"Thanks to our sources, we felt the drop was going to be somewhere close to Grosse Ile Airport. But we didn't know where," Agent Waters said. It was still hard to think of Kat's dad that way. "Not until Kathleen confirmed it was Dom and turned on her tracking device."

"Dom went south because the Hole in the Wall is monitored," Kat added. "He knew he'd get picked up right away, out in a storm and all."

We sat around the *Southern Comfort*'s cabin—Kat, me, Dad, Agent Waters and Officer Murphy. Kat was beside me, holding my hand. My heart rate was still up from the kiss she'd given me—right in front of everyone—when she arrived. Her Southern hug became a repeat of the previous night's. When we came up for air, I saw both of our dads smiling. *Crazy.*

"We never got a chance to put trackers on the Oleg boats. Things happened too fast. When Kathleen texted, I was already at the island's airport. With her signal, we moved into position."

"I knew it was Dom driving the whole time," she admitted.

"Once he went past the yacht club, we were sure he was headed to the Herons' place. We knew he was there often. So I already had men standing by." He took a sip of coffee before he went on. "Kathleen tells me you met Troy Heron at the party."

I nodded.

"Daddy brought the Herons in. But he thinks they're clean. It looks like Dom acted alone."

I looked at Agent Waters. "Did you know Oleg was smuggling people into the States?" I asked. "Or were you just after the drugs?"

"The human smuggling is what brought me here. We've watched that group for months. We caught one guy already."

"The one you told me about," Kat said.

"We're after the guys at the top." Agent Walker paused. "We picked up Dom's 'guests' once they were out of sight. My people are taking their places."

"If you guys were after the human smugglers, how did you know about the drugs?" I asked.

"We didn't. Not until yesterday. That new network I mentioned last night? It was key in putting the pieces together."

Kat's dad pointed at Nate's father. "The drugs are Murphy's case."

Nate's father had been sitting quietly beside my dad. Now he picked up the story.

"A week ago the RCMP got a tip. Quebec Ecstasy, coming through our area. Destination New York, with a possible Boblo tie-in. No idea of the who or how, but we did know the shipment was leaving from Grosse Ile Airport last night. That's when the tower guy goes home," Officer Murphy said.

"Someone was getting the drugs to the airport over the river. We've all been watching Customs, the RCMP, everyone. We knew the river was key, but nothing flagged. Time was up. Tonight was it. We knew they had to move."

"So you and Agent Waters joined forces?" I asked.

"All the groups involved only got clearance to share intel over the new network in the last twenty-four hours," Officer Murphy said. "Most of us don't work together very often. Or very easily." He laughed.

"The new network was key. When we shared what we knew, everything fell into place," Agent Waters said.

Officer Murphy looked at my dad, who'd also been sitting quietly. "Do you want to tell him the rest, Butch?" he asked.

Butch? As in my dad? What would he know about any of this?

My dad stood up. "Let's go over to the shed." I could tell he was trying not to smile.

I hadn't been within ten meters of the shed in months. I could hear a buzzing sound as I got closer.

Then Dad opened the shed door... and I couldn't believe my eyes.

Inside were floor-to-ceiling wires, with computers and monitors everywhere.

Officer Murphy put his hand on my shoulder. "Your dad is the mastermind behind our new network, Tom. He's been working on it for months."

"I couldn't tell a soul, Tom," Dad said. "The RCMP hired me to design it. I know the river, and I know all the local marine communications systems."

I could hear the pride in his voice, and I almost lost it right there.

"We used this old shed because I could set everything up and you wouldn't know I was doing something extra. It's a perfect location for the hub." He paused. "I had a hell of a time keeping you away from this shed though."

You have no idea.

"When they saw I could run the whole thing, not just build it, Joe gave me the contract. He's my RCMP contact."

Joe. The guy on the phone.

"Anyway, it's a full-time job, keeping this hub running." He looked around the shed. "So I guess you're going to have to run the marina on your own next summer."

"What?" I must have heard wrong.

"I'll be able to afford a manager," Dad said. "Consider yourself hired."

Kat and I held hands, swinging our feet as we sat on the *Southern Comfort*'s swimming platform.

"It's good your dad's helping Oleg," I said.

"Dom giving evidence will help for sure. And he seems truly sorry," Kat said. "It sounds like Mr. Oleg was really hard on him. Putting all that pressure on him about school. Cutting off his money when Dom thinks money is everything.

I think he was desperate." Kat squeezed my hand. "At least they're talking now. Dad's booked some counseling."

"I just wish I knew why Oleg's always been such a jerk to me. Thank God he doesn't know we were part of him getting caught." Agent Waters had managed to keep our names out of the proceedings so far.

"I have some leads on that," Kat said. "Do you remember when Dom was arrested? He was mumbling about someone being right about him being dumb?"

I thought back. "Yeah. I figured he was talking about his dad."

"No. He was talking about you."

"Me?" I was instantly mad. "I never called him dumb. Not until this year maybe. And never to his face!"

"He told Dad last night that you were in daycare with him when he first moved here. You were little, and you told all the kids his name was Dumb instead of Dom. They teased him. Guess he never got over it."

"I stopped going to daycare when I was *two*! Dad took over the marina, and I stayed home. I wouldn't even know what *dumb* meant! It was so crazy I could barely wrap my head around it. I probably just repeated what I thought he said."

"Maybe when things are better you can talk to him about it." Kat moved closer to me. "Anyway, I'm done talking about Dom Oleg. I can think of better things to do." She pulled me in for a kiss.

With Kat beside me, and the sun a gold ball sinking low across the river, I quickly forgot about Oleg. I was ready for some smooth sailing and some brighter horizons. My ship had definitely come in.

Martha Brack Martin is an award-winning teacher-librarian in the southern Ontario town of LaSalle, near Windsor. After twenty-five years as a teacher (seventeen of them as a teacher librarian), she still gets a thrill out of getting kids excited about reading and finding just the right book for each person. She was dared by a colleague a few years ago to put *Book Babe* on her business card and now revels in the title. The creator of a number of Book Babe Teacher Guides, and author of four nonfiction books for children, she frequently facilitates workshops on children's literature, teaching with technology, and librarianship. This is her first novel.

Titles in the Series

orca soundings

**Another Miserable
Love Song**
Brooke Carter

Back
Norah McClintock

Bang
Norah McClintock

Battle of the Bands
K.L. Denman

Big Guy
Robin Stevenson

Bike Thief
Rita Feutl

Blue Moon
Marilyn Halvorson

B Negative
Vicki Grant

Breaking Point
Lesley Choyce

Breathing Fire
Sarah Yi-Mei Tsiang

Breathless
Pam Withers

Bull Rider
Marilyn Halvorson

Bull's Eye
Sarah N. Harvey

Cellular
Ellen Schwartz

Charmed
Carrie Mac

Chill
Colin Frizzell

Comeback
Vicki Grant

Coming Clean
Jeff Ross

Crash
Lesley Choyce

Crush
Carrie Mac

Cuts Like a Knife
Darlene Ryan

Damage
Robin Stevenson

A Dark Truth
Jeff Ross

The Darwin Expedition
Diane Tullson

Dead Run
Sean Rodman

Dead-End Job
Vicki Grant

Deadly
Sarah N. Harvey

Death Wind
William Bell

Down
Norah McClintock

Enough
Mary Jennifer Payne

Exit Point
Laura Langston

Exposure
Patricia Murdoch

Fallout
Nikki Tate

Fastback Beach
Shirlee Smith Matheson

Final Crossing
Sean Rodman

First Time
Meg Tilly

Foolproof
Diane Tullson

Grind
Eric Walters

Hannah's Touch
Laura Langston

The Hemingway Tradition
Kristin Butcher

Hit Squad
James Heneghan

Home Invasion
Monique Polak

Homecoming
Diane Dakers

House Party
Eric Walters

I.D.
Vicki Grant

Impact
James C. Dekker

Infiltration
Sean Rodman

In the Woods
Robin Stevenson

Jacked
Carrie Mac

Juice
Eric Walters

Kicked Out
Beth Goobie

Knifepoint
Alex Van Tol

Last Ride
Laura Langston

Learning to Fly
Paul Yee

Lockdown
Diane Tullson

Masked
Norah McClintock

Middle Row
Sylvia Olsen

My Side
Norah McClintock

My Time as Caz Hazard
Tanya Lloyd Kyi

Night Terrors
Sean Rodman

No More Pranks
Monique Polak

No Problem
Dayle Campbell Gaetz

Off the Grid
Lesley Choyce

One More Step
Sheree Fitch

One Way
Norah McClintock

Outback
Robin Stevenson

Overdrive
Eric Walters

Pain & Wastings
Carrie Mac

Picture This
Norah McClintock

Plastic
Sarah N. Harvey

Rat
Lesley Choyce

Reaction
Lesley Choyce

Redline
Alex Van Tol

Refuge Cove
Lesley Choyce

Responsible
Darlene Ryan

Riley Park
Diane Tullson

Riot Act
Diane Tullson

River Traffic
Martha Brack Martin

Rock Star
Adrian Chamberlain

Running the Risk
Lesley Choyce

Saving Grace
Darlene Ryan

Scam
Lesley Choyce

Scum
James C. Dekker

Sea Change
Diane Tullson

Shallow Grave
Alex Van Tol

Shattered
Sarah N. Harvey

Skylark
Sara Cassidy

Sleight of Hand
Natasha Deen

Snitch
Norah McClintock

Something Girl
Beth Goobie

Spiral
K.L. Denman

Sticks and Stones
Beth Goobie

Stuffed
Eric Walters

Tagged
Eric Walters

Tap Out
Sean Rodman

Tell
Norah McClintock

Thunderbowl
Lesley Choyce

Tough Trails
Irene Morck

Triggered
Vicki Grant

The Trouble with Liberty
Kristin Butcher

Truth
Tanya Lloyd Kyi

Under Threat
Robin Stevenson

Viral
Alex Van Tol

Wave Warrior
Lesley Choyce

The Way Back
Carrie Mac

Who Owns Kelly Paddik?
Beth Goobie

Yellow Line
Sylvia Olsen

Zee's Way
Kristin Butcher

orca soundings

For more information on all the books
in the Orca Soundings series, please visit
www.orcabook.com.